Witch-in-
Training
Spelling
Trouble

Collins

An imprint of HarperCollins*Publishers*

07206

Also by Maeve Friel.
Witch-in-Training: Flying Lessons

Coming soon:
Witch-in-Training: Charming or What?
Witch-in-Training: Brewing Up

Other Roaring Good Reads from Collins

Mister Skip *by Michael Morpurgo*
Daisy May *by Jean Ure*
The Witch's Tears *by Jenny Nimmo*
Spider McDrew *by Alan Durant*
Dazzling Danny *by Jean Ure*

Witch-in-Training

Spelling Trouble

Maeve Friel

Illustrated by Nathan Reed

ROARING GOOD READS

Collins

An imprint of HarperCollins*Publishers*

First published by Collins in 2003
Collins is an imprint of HarperCollins Publishers Ltd
77-85 Fulham Palace Road, Hammersmith, London W6 8JB

The HarperCollins website address is www.fireandwater.com

1 3 5 7 9 8 6 4 2

ISBN 0 00 713342 1

Printed and bound in England by
Clays Ltd, St Ives plc

Chapter One

Jessica Diamond found out that she was a witch on her tenth birthday. She started broom-flying lessons at once with the legendary witch trainer, Miss Strega, and soon afterwards passed her Flying Test (despite a nearly catastrophic encounter with a tearaway goblin). Now she was about to begin her Spelling Lessons.

Miss Strega's shop was founded in 991. It was an old-fashioned hardware shop, tucked in between the estate agent's and the toy shop. If anyone peered in through the window they could see what a heap of junk

it sold: There were hurricane lamps and mousetraps and flypapers dangling from hooks high above a stack of iron cooking pots; and untidy balls of string which unwound themselves and got caught up in broomsticks and bird scarers. But hardly anyone ever went inside and if they did Miss Strega shooed them away, saying she was closing up early.

When Jessica arrived after school that afternoon, she discovered the place was even messier than usual. It looked as if a tornado had just rushed through it. There were cauldrons, cobwebby crates and three-legged stools lying all over the floor. Dozens of dusty books were scattered on the counter beneath a pile of flying helmets.

And Miss Strega herself seemed to have been blown into the cupboard under the stairs, for she suddenly emerged draped from head to toe in witches' cloaks.

"What on earth has happened?" Jessica asked, dismounting from her broom and rushing to disentangle Miss Strega. "Have you been burgled?"

"Not at all, my little lamb's lettuce!" exclaimed Miss Strega. "Perish the thought. I'm just having a good sort-out. We can revise your renaming skills at the same time."

"My *renaming* skills?" Jessica frowned.

Miss Strega pushed Felicity, her fat ginger cat, off a stool and set down armfuls of cloaks. "As you now know, Jessica," she said, tapping the side of her long nose, "I am the Official Storekeeper of the Members of Witches World Wide, the W3. My shop has to be a highly undercover secret operation so I make the shop look as uninviting as possible to ordinary people. Even so, once in a blue moon, some chump blunders in looking for garden shears or a packet of parsley seeds, so…"

"I know," said Jessica, "you rename things so that they think they really *are* in a hardware shop before you chase them out. Like you put the Teenage Slugs in a drawer marked Ten-Amp plugs."

"Exactly," agreed Miss Strega. "There are two Spelling Programmes involved – Noquan and Sablit."

Jessica's eyes opened wide.

"NOQUAN stands for Not-Quite-an-Anagram. SABLIT – Sounds-a-Bit-Like-It. You'll soon get the hang of them. Pop up on your broom and follow me."

The back wall of the shop was covered from top to bottom in wooden drawers with brass handles and spidery handwritten labels.

"Look at that, for example," she said, pointing at a label that read Parsley Seeds. "What do you think I really keep in that drawer?"

Jessica knitted her brow. "Is it Sablit? Pa's Sleigh Beads. No, that doesn't make any sense."

Miss Strega stroked her long chin. "Try Noquan."

Jessica allowed the letters to swim around in her mind. "Could it be a Sleepy Dress? A magic dress that makes whoever wears it fall asleep?"

"I can see you are going to be a whiz at Noquan," Miss Strega chuckled. "What about Ten-inch Nails?"

"Oh, I remember that one from before. They're Snails' Antennae."

"Grate Polish?"

"Gnat's Spittle."

"Slide Rules?"

"Yeuch," said Jessica as she worked it out. "That must be Snails' Drool."

"Tickety-boo. Now, let's do it the other way round. Where could you put the Dragon Spears?"

"Behind the Garden Shears?"

"Good girl. A pot of Happy Dream?"

"Nappy Cream?"

"Lungs of Skunk?"

"Sink Plungers," Jessica grinned. "But what are they all for?"

"I was just coming to that," said Miss Strega, "but first I'll make us a stiff brew while you tidy away all this clutter. I'm sure you'll have no difficulty in working out where everything goes."

While Miss Strega stirred her brew, Jessica tidied up the shop. She was just putting the last of the Serpent Tears in the drawer labelled Secateurs when a book on the counter caught her eye.

As everybody knows, it's very difficult not to pick up a book with a good cover. However, the book that caught Jessica's eye did *not* have a good cover. In fact it did not have a cover at all. It was very grubby and spattered with multicoloured stains like a well-used cookery book. Indeed, as Jessica discovered when she riffled through the pages, *Spelling Made Easy* was a sort of recipe book but for very odd dishes like Astronomical Turnovers and Vanishing Cream. She flipped the pages back to the Introduction.

"Spelling is easy," she read aloud, "but the secret of *good* Spelling is in the Mingling."

"Absolutely!" said Miss Strega, giving her cauldron a resounding smack with a wooden spoon. The sudden noise gave Berkeley, Jessica's night-in-gale mascot, a

terrible shock. She had
been having an
afternoon nap in
Jessica's pocket but
now soared up to the
ceiling rafters with a
warning "hu-eet, hu-eet".

Miss Strega pretended not to notice and
went on. "As you say, the art of Spelling,
Jessica, is in the Mingling."

Jessica read the sentence again. "Actually,
I don't understand it at all. What exactly is
Mingling?"

"As luck would have it, Jessica," said Miss
Strega as she hopped up on her high stool,
"Mingling is the next topic of our Spelling
Lessons."

Chapter Two

Jessica sat cross-legged on the counter and laid her broom carefully beside her. Berkeley fluttered down from the ceiling and perched on her shoulder. Felicity jumped up on to the counter too, arched her back, stretched, circled three times and finally settled down on Jessica's lap, purring loudly.

Miss Strega rapped her knuckles on *Spelling Made Easy*. "If you are all sure you're comfortable, I'll begin. There are several Spelling techniques that you will have to learn as part of your training but..."

"How many?" Jessica interrupted.

"Well, there's Spelling With Brews and Potions; Spelling With and Without Wands and Chanting to name but three. Mingling is a basic craft when we use Spelling With Brews and Potions and that's our lesson for today. I'll make one of the Potions from *Spelling Made Easy* to show you how it works. It's a rather old textbook, as you can see, and a bit *old-fashioned*, but it does include several timeless Spellings..."

"*You* are not at all old-fashioned, Miss Strega," Jessica interrupted, "even though you must be very old."

Miss Strega stroked her chin very thoughtfully. She opened the book at Starter

Brews. "This is a good one," she said and she began to read aloud: "Alphabet Soup: first rub your cauldron with a light film of oil. Throw in a handful of letters of the alphabet, a few commas and full stops. Season as required with question marks or exclamation marks and bring to the boil. Correct stirring is essential or you will end up with a soup of meaningless words with no magic properties at all."

"But what is it *for*?" asked Jessica.

Miss Strega sighed loudly. "Do concentrate, Jessica. Obviously, the Alphabet Soup Spell is used to plant a word or an idea in someone's head."

"What sort of idea?"

"Say, for example, that someone is doing something really irritating and you want them to stop—"

"Like what?"

"Anything irritating!" Miss Strega sounded rather snappish. "So, you grease your cauldron, like so, throw in a handful of the letters of the alphabet and—"

"Yes, but which letters?"

"Moonrays and marrowbones, Jessica! Any or all of them will do. It doesn't matter a whit. It's the way you Mingle that puts the right words in the person's brain."

"But I don't understand what the Mingling is… and how does the person know what to think?"

Miss Strega sighed and drank a thimbleful of her own stiff brew. "Now pay attention," she ordered. "I'm starting to Mingle." Holding her left hand behind her back like a television cook, she extravagantly sprinkled a few exclamation marks into the cauldron.

"Now take the feather of a long-eared owl…"
"Does it have to be a long-eared owl?
Would a short-eared one not work?"

"...and draw it backwards and forwards over your soup like this." Miss Strega closed her eyes and drew the long feather rapidly over the soup. "Backwards and forwards, figures-of-eight," she chanted, "round and about, a criss and a cross, then loop the loop."

"Do you have to close your eyes?" Jessica asked. "How many times must you..."

Jessica's voice trailed off into silence. All of a sudden, the words

STOP INTERRUPTING!!!

had popped up in her brain and were flashing on and off like warning lights. She covered her face with her hands and peered through her fingers.

Miss Strega was doing her best not to laugh. She had covered her chin with her hand and pressed her lips together but her shoulders were shaking up and down and tears were rolling down her cheeks.

"May *I* try to Mingle?" Jessica asked, all polite.

"Of course, my dear."

Jessica lightly oiled a cauldron. She threw in a handful of letters and seasoned her mixture with a single exclamation mark.

She began to Mingle, doing the figures-of-eight routine, the side-to-side, the round and abouts, the crissing and crossing, then looping the loop.

Miss Strega's shoulders stopped shaking. Her nose turned a little red and she abruptly started to inspect her finger nails. "Was I really showing off, Jess?" she said, sheepishly.

"Yes," said Jessica, "you were."

And they both began to cackle so long and so loudly that Berkeley rose off Jessica's shoulder in alarm and Felicity leapt off Jessica's lap and dashed out through the cat flap.

"By the hooting of Minerva's owl, Jessica," said Miss Strega when they had caught their

breath, "I can't remember the last time a witch-in-training got the better of me like that. But," she added hastily as Jessica turned a little pink, "before you get too bigheaded, remember that you have a long way to go before you get your Spelling Certificate."

Jessica groaned. "More tests?"

"Of course." Miss Strega picked up the copy of *Spelling Made Easy*. "For your homework, I want you to learn all the Spells in Chapters One and Two. Word-perfect, please, with Mingling actions as recommended."

Chapter Three

The following day when Jessica flew in for her next Spelling Lesson, she was surprised to see a notice in the shop window.

EVERYTHING HALF PRICE

Inside, the walls were covered in a blizzard of notices and special offers.

Unicorn Hairs, 3 for the price of 2
Stardust, Economy Pack,
Now only 4 groats

"Oh goody," thought Jessica, "Miss Strega is having a sale. I wonder if I have enough pocket money for a new cloak."

Jessica had made her cloak from a black plastic bin liner and it was looking very much the worse for wear. She was hunting for a new one in her size when Miss Strega appeared from her private apartment with a large cauldron of brew.

"Mmm, that smells yummy," said Jessica. "What is it?"

"Cold Smelly Voles," said Miss Strega setting it down on the counter. "It's for my customers. Shoppers tend to spend more when they get free samples. I've made up some nibbles too."

"You mean things like cocktail sausages and cubes of cheese?"

"That sort of thing: bewitching jambarollies, spellbinding munchies," said Miss Strega, pouring herself a thimbleful of brew. "But especially Cold Smelly Voles. Cheers! By the way, are you looking for something?"

"Yes," said Jessica, picking up a lovely satin cloak with a velvet trim. "I thought I might get myself a new cloak."

"Nonsense," said Miss Strega, putting it back on the pile. "You mustn't worry your enchanting little head about a new cloak just yet. A bright young witch like you needs to learn how to Spell first."

Jessica frowned. Sometimes Miss Strega sounded *exactly* like her mother.

The news that Miss Strega was holding a sale had spread like wildfire among the W3. Soon there were witches flying in from north, south, east and west to stock up on all the cut-price bargains. The Broom Cupboard and the Cloak Room were full to bursting with broomsticks and cloaks. As the

witches shouted out their orders, Jessica
whizzed around on her broom trying to
guess what Miss Strega might have written
on the labels.

"Three Pokes of Fever!"

"Four Lungs of Skunk!"

"Have you got any of those new Goblin Deterrents?"

Jessica was completely baffled by the Goblin Deterrents.

Meanwhile Miss Strega ladled out tumblers of Cold Smelly Voles to each newcomer. Little groups of friends sat on the three-legged stools, sipping their drinks and swapping news.

"What a marvellous pick-me-up this is, especially after a long flight," they all agreed.

"Clearly cold and seriously smelly."

"Yuck," thought Jessica. Although, when she had a sip of Cold Smelly Voles she found it tasted rather deliciously of lemons and cloves. Miss Strega was brewing in Sablit.

The party – for that is what it sounded like – was in full noisy swing when, suddenly, the door was flung open and in hurried a very interesting-looking witch. In the first place, she was wearing a *white* cloak with red cross- trimmings and an extraordinary pair of knee-length boots with a design of flying bats. She had a stethoscope hung around her neck and a medicine bag swinging from the end of her broom.

"Dr Krank! How lovely to see you!" Miss Strega exclaimed. "What can we do for you this evening?"

"Oh my dear Miss Strega," Dr Krank replied, "thank goodness your shop is still open. You won't believe the hubble and bubble I've got myself into. My General Purpose This-will-fix-it Brew has burnt dry! When I flew in to my surgery this afternoon, what did I find but smoke pouring out of the windows, all the cats coughing and a hole the size of a dinner plate in the bottom of the first-aid cauldron. I'll have to start a new brew from scratch."

Miss Strega tut-tutted sympathetically. "Would you like to have Jessica, my witch-in-training, as your personal assistant? If you give her your list of ingredients, she'll mingle it all up for you. We've just been learning the art of Mingling." Miss Strega lifted her long-eared owl's feather and began to draw it over the cauldron of Alphabet Soup which was still sitting on the counter from the previous day.

Dr Krank looked rather doubtfully at Jessica. "A witch-in-training? I don't suppose she can Spell. Youngsters never can these days."

"Of course she can Spell. She'll Spell whatever you ask her."

Jessica looked at Miss Strega in horror.

"Very well," Dr Krank commanded. "Spell..." She hesitated for a moment.

Miss Strega continued distractedly waving her feather over the cauldron.

"I've got it." Dr Krank snapped her fingers. "Spell Cheery-ade."

"Brilliant," thought Jessica. That was one of her homework Spellings. It sounded good fun:

"One guffaw, two grins,
A can of laughter, giggles (two tins),
Blend with beeswax, two large packs.
Now rub the lotion behind the ear,
Your bad mood will disappear."

"Bravo!" Miss Strega beamed with pride at her pupil and winked.

"Charming," chorused the customers, raising their glasses of Cold Smelly Voles.

Even Dr Krank smiled as she selected one of the largest black cauldrons and blew the dust off it.

"Enchanting. A classic spell for cheering people up," she agreed. "So, Jessica, I'd be delighted if you could help me fetch the ingredients, but I'll do my own Mingling, thank you very much. Here is the list of ingredients for my General Purpose This-will-fix-it Brew. I'll need a sieveful of

Stardust and a dozen Milk Teeth to start with."

While Dr Krank toiled over her cauldron, stirring round and round and roundabout, Jessica zoomed about the shop until her head was spinning, pulling out cobwebby drawers and rooting among the dusty cupboards for a Beloved Teddy Bear, Mystic Biscuits, Buttercup Dew, the Scent of Snow, a Baby's Chuckle. She even found the Goblin Deterrent, cleverly renamed Oblong Detergents.

Dr Krank's cauldron foamed and fizzed, bubbled and boiled, filling the shop with the most wonderful aroma. At last she laid down her feather and called for her broom and cloak.

"I think that ought to fix most of the complaints I come across in a day's work. And now, I must fly. Jessica, will you help me load this on to my bezom."

Wobbling a little under its weight, Jessica heaved the brimming cauldron up on to the doctor's broomstick.

Dr Krank steadied herself for take-off, fast-forwarded through the door, and with a final wave, flew off into the night, scattering droplets of brew behind her.

When the last witch had left, Jessica helped Miss Strega count the money in the till.

Miss Strega seemed very pleased with herself. "I hope you remember that recipe," she remarked as she totted up the groats and the maravedis. "Dr Krank is famous throughout the W3 for her medicinal brews. They are jolly good and smell divinely. Naturally, she wouldn't dream of using those Eye of Newt or Lung of Skunk concoctions."

"I was just wondering," Jessica probed, "when you were Mingling your feather over the Alphabet Soup, if perhaps *you* planted the Cheery-ade thought in Dr Krank's brain?"

Miss Strega's hand flew to her chin. "Great honking goose feathers, Jessica, I don't know where you get some of your ideas. Now, let's finish the last of the Cold Smelly Voles and have a quick moon-vault before supper!"

Chapter Four

"Whoops," shouted Jessica as she hurtled through the shop door. "Gangway!" Somehow she had hit the Fast-Forward twig of her broomstick instead of the Pause control. Miss Strega only just got out of her way before Jessica collided with a display of new brooms, toppled over a stack of cauldrons and sent Felicity flying off the counter.

"Moonrays and marrowbones!" exclaimed Miss Strega, scratching the cat between the ears. "There's no call for that kind of rough behaviour."

"I'm so sorry," said Jessica. "I must have pressed the wrong twig by mistake."

Miss Strega sniffed noisily and reached for her broomstick. "We'd best get started. Today we are doing Transformation Spells, using the Wand Method."

The lesson went badly from the very beginning. Miss Strega was in an awful grump and Jessica couldn't do anything right.

"Don't hold your wand like that!" Miss Strega objected as Jessica demonstrated her wand-whooshing to Berkeley. Or she complained, "Stop lolling on your broom, back straight, knees tucked up."

Later, while they were waiting for an experiment to work – Jessica was attempting to change a coin into a chocolate drop – she tut-tutted, "This is taking far too long."

"This is horrible," thought Jessica.

Miss Strega popped the chocolate drop in her mouth. "Changing money into sweets is all very well but Transformation Spells are mostly used to transform living things. For example, say a huge flock of rooks were chasing you on your broomstick, what could you change them into?"

Jessica thought hard. "A feather pillow?" she joked.

Miss Strega did *not* smile. "On the other hand, you might find yourself in a spot of bother and decide to turn *yourself* into something else. Could you give me an example of that?"

"Perhaps if I was on the Milky Way, and a huge fire-breathing dragon was heading straight for me and I was going to get run over, I could turn myself into a red traffic light and the dragon would have to stop."

"Woolly walrus tusks!" groaned Miss Strega. "What do you think your Ducking and Diving twigs are for? Any witch worthy of her flying licence can nip out of the way of a dragon without having to do a Transformation Spell. Come on, think!"

"Maybe, if I was in a room with a very bad-tempered monster, I could change myself into a rug."

"And get stamped and trodden on?" Miss Strega raised an eyebrow.

"Maybe," Jessica said to herself – but not out loud – and with a casual wave of her wand, "maybe if I was in a room with a very bad-tempered monster, I could change *her* into a wasp."

Miss Strega's broom suddenly fell to the floor with a loud clatter. The space where Miss Strega had been was empty. She had vanished.

Jessica's mouth flew open. Felicity's eyes blazed two warning orange beacons.

An angry buzzing noise was coming from one of the small panes of the shop window.

Jessica tiptoed towards it. To her horror, the noise was coming from a wasp, a wasp with a familiar-looking face.

"I'm so sorry, Miss Strega. I didn't mean to turn you into a wasp."

"Yes, you did," Miss Strega buzzed huffily.

"Please don't sting me."

"You know, Jessica, there are times when you have about as much sense as a pumpkin."

The wasp hovered over Jessica's head for a moment, then flitted across the room and dropped down on the counter. Her front legs waved rapidly.

Jessica felt herself blushing. Her cheeks blazed red. In fact, her whole body began to feel very odd. She began to inflate like a balloon. Her face and arms and legs grew rounder and rounder until she was a large round ball.

"You've turned me into a pumpkin!" she protested.

"Yes, I have," agreed the wasp, "a pumpkin with a very lop-sided embarrassed smile – as well it might."

"I really am very sorry," Jessica apologized.

Miss Wasp Strega lowered her front legs. "Well, I apologize too if I was a bit waspish." She buzzed over and sat on the floor beside Jessica Pumpkin.

"Now what shall we do?" said Jessica. "How long do these Spells last?"

"Who knows?" Miss Strega raised her waspy shoulders and let them drop. "Bad-tempered Spells are very difficult to predict. Our only hope is that a customer drops in who can un-Transform us. In the meantime, let's hope Felicity or Berkeley don't try to swat me or nibble bits of you."

Chapter Five

It seemed like hours before anyone came to their rescue. Miss Strega hid in a little hollow at the top of Jessica's head and soon fell asleep. Jessica watched people rushing past on the High Street. Nobody even glanced at the hardware shop. Bored, miserable and unable to move, Jessica waited and waited. Berkeley kept her spirits up by perching on her pumpkinny shoulder and loudly singing, "Don't give up, hu-eet, hu-eet, hu-eet."

At long last, the door latch clicked.

"Yoo-hoo. Anyone at home? I think I must have left my owl feather here on the night of the sale."

Miss Strega buzzed excitedly and flew out of her hidey-hole. "Oh Jess, that sounds like our old friend, the witch doctor, Dr Krank."

Unfortunately, Miss Strega did not sound like herself, at least not to Dr Krank who was none too pleased by this pesky buzzing, humming, whirring nuisance flitting around her head. She pinged the counter bell to let Miss Strega know she had a

customer, picked up a Spell book and
swatted at the wasp.

"Stop! That's Miss Strega," Jessica shouted
at the top of her voice. But under the
pumpkin Spell, she couldn't be heard at all.
After all, pumpkins can't speak.

Dr Krank lashed out again with the rolled-up Spell book. "Miss Strega," she yelled, "Come here at once. I'm under attack."

"I *am* here!" Miss Strega yelled back as she zoomed higher out of Dr Krank's reach. "I'm under a Spell."

Dr Krank impatiently banged the counter with the side of her broomstick and rang the bell again, but much more loudly.

"Miss Strega!" she shouted, shooing away Felicity who was mewing loudly and doing figures-of-eight around her legs. "Where the dickens are you?" She stared around the shop with a baffled expression. "Now where can I have left that owl feather?" she muttered. Then she caught sight of Jessica.

Jessica gave her an embarrassed smile.

"What a very life like pumpkin," Dr Krank

remarked, smiling back. "It reminds me of someone I met recently."

Miss Strega buzzed back down from the ceiling where she had taken refuge.

"Dr Krank," she whirred, "that is Jessica, my witch-in-training. Don't you see we're under a Spell?"

"Not you again!" Dr Krank crossly swiped Miss Strega with her broomstick. This time she did not miss. Miss Strega fell to the floor in a daze.

It was Berkeley who saved the day. As Dr Krank remounted her broom to depart, Berkeley flew off Jessica's shoulder, perched on the door latch and urgently began to sing.

Dr Krank dismounted. She listened intently to the song, looked at the dizzy wasp, then

at the embarrassed smile of the pumpkin and tapped her nose.

"I see," she said, "you two are having some Spelling Trouble. Let's see what I can do to undo the damage." She set her medicine bag on the counter and took out a small round silver globe.

Miss Strega, who had struggled back on to her feet, flew up in the air buzzing frantically.

"Miss Strega," Dr Krank sighed, "would you please stop whirring and humming. It's terribly distracting. You'd better have your voices back." She pulled her wand out of her bag and lightly struck the pumpkin and the wasp three times. Then she intoned:

"*Gorgonzola, genie of glitches,*

Restore the tongues of these two witches."

"Thank you," whispered Jessica hoarsely, looking more embarrassed than ever.

Miss Strega raised her front legs and rubbed her face where she felt her ears ought to be. "By the screeching of peacocks and the racket of rooks, I shall not be sorry to give up buzzing."

Dr Krank chuckled. "The flitting is quite annoying too," she said as she lifted Jessica and placed her on the counter. "Come and sit here atop Jessica and I'll explain the Withershins Ball Manoeuvre."

"Mmmm, the old Withershins trick." Miss Strega pursed her lips. "Maybe that would work."

"No maybe about it!" Dr Krank retorted. She placed the silver ball on her palm and held it out so that the whole shop was reflected in miniature on the surface.

Jessica could see herself, very orange and very round, in the mirror world, with Miss

Wasp Strega and Berkeley sitting on top of her head. Behind her she could see the topsy-turvy shop with cauldrons and three-legged stools dangling from the ceiling hooks.

"Withershins," Dr Krank explained to Jessica, "is an old word that means going contrariwise, like a clock's hands going backwards."

"Or a supersonic broomstick flying against the rotation of the earth?" Jessica suggested.

"Precisely. What a clever little thing you are."

Miss Strega cleared her throat.

"So," Dr Krank continued, "I will make the ball turn back to the time when you made your spells and, hey presto, you'll be back to your usual selves. Expect to feel a little disenchanted as the Spell wears off," she added. "You may be a bit headachy – but you'll be fine in a couple of hours. I'll drop back later to see how you both are."

Dr Krank's Withershins Ball began to twist and turn anticlockwise on her palm, so slowly that at first it didn't seem to be moving at all.

Jessica could see herself, still propped on the counter. The ball began to spin faster.

Now Jessica was on the floor again. She felt the tickle of Miss Strega's wings as she slept in Jessica's hollow.

The ball spun even faster.

Jessica felt herself shrinking as her round orangeness wore off. She sprouted arms and legs again.

Somewhere, far away, she could hear Dr Krank chanting:

"Withershins, Withershins,
Thrice again and thrice again."

Now, in the Withershins Ball, she was standing by the window looking at a furious buzzing wasp.

"Don't sting me," she was saying.

The revolutions of the ball became slower. Then, with one final orbit, it leapt into the air and disappeared.

Miss Strega and Jessica were alone in the shop, observing a gold coin slowly transform itself into a chocolate drop.

"Excellent Spelling, my little hunny-bunny," Miss Strega announced as she popped the sweet in her mouth. "I think you are just about ready for your Spelling Test. But let's call it a night now, shall we? I can't think why but suddenly I'm feeling a little out of sorts."

Chapter Six

Jessica's Spelling Test was to take place in the library at Coven Garden, the headquarters of the W3. She had taken her Flying Test on the roof there but had never been inside the building. It was very posh.

She dismounted her broom on the steps in front of the tall arched doorway and nervously walked into the reception hall. It was a perfectly round room with a mosaic floor in the pattern of a huge spider's web. The words *Witches World Wide Wishing the*

World Well ran around the outer rim of the
web. The walls were covered from top to
bottom with large portraits of members of
the W3. The largest of all, opposite the front
door, was a painting of a witch mounted on
her broomstick and wearing full ceremonial

garb; a broadly striped purple and green sash, a heavy velvet cloak and a traditional pointy hat. She looked very scary, peering down at Jessica over her half-moon glasses.

Jessica shuddered. "That's the awful Miss Shar Pintake of BR(EATH)," she reminded Berkeley, "the examiner at my Flying Test. Let's hope she doesn't take the Spelling Test as well."

Jessica gloomily climbed the marble stairs and followed the signs for the library. It was a long high-ceilinged room, its bookcases crammed with Spell books, Charm manuals and Witch history. There were antique maps and globes of the Earth and the Heavens as well as a dreary collection of Early Irish cauldrons.

Jessica was squinting at a framed copy of the Deed of Surrender after the Bezom Wars when she heard the dreaded sound of someone sucking her teeth. As she turned around, Miss

Shar Pintake announced, "Jessica Diamond, your Spelling Test starts now."

The first written tests were simple. She had to do a few exercises in Renaming.

Candidates may use either Noquan or Sablit.

What would you expect to find behind drawers labelled:
a.   Crockery (SOLD)
b.   Low Watt Bulbs
c.   Steel Trowels
d.   Knitting Needles?

Well, that was no problem. Jessica filled in the boxes.

a. ....Crocks of Gold
b. ....Wallaby Toes

c. ....Troll Squeals
d. ....Kittens' Piddle

Then there was a question about the ingredients for the basic brew.

> Which of the following should never be included in a General Purpose Medicinal Brew?
>
> The Moan of the North Wind, a Baby's Chuckle, a Sieveful of Stardust, Buttercup Dew

Easy peasy.

It was the final task in the practical tests that caused the problem.

"And now," Shar Pintake's nostrils flared as if she had just noticed a really bad smell, "I'd like you to do a Transformation Spell, by

means of a chant. Wands are not allowed."
She clicked her fingers at the foaming mini-
cauldron on her desk. A card rose slowly
from its misty depths and flew across the
room into Jessica's hand.

It said:

Change something you love into something horrid.

Jessica groaned. She had hardly glanced
at Transformation Spells since that disastrous
experience with Miss Strega. She had

certainly never bothered to learn the Love-to-Hate Spell, thinking it very unlikely that she would ever want to risk changing something she loved into something nasty. There was nothing for it but to make up a chant of her own.

She took a deep breath and plunged headlong into a rhyme, like someone splashing off on a cross-country run wishing it was already over.

"Three Chocolate Mice,
Three Chocolate Mice,
See how they melt,
See how they melt,
They all run into the tablecloth,
It soaks them up with the chicken broth,
The gravy stains and the coffee froth..."

Jessica stopped dead. How on earth was she going to end this nonsense? Shar Pintake would want something more horrid than a dirty tablecloth.

"Cloth... Broth... Froth... To the disgust of a hovering moth? To the delight of a black-eyed Goth?" she muttered under her breath.

Shar Pintake was staring at her over her half-moon glasses. "Speak up, girl!"

Jessica could have wept. "Why did I not do more homework?" she thought. "All those nights I've wasted vaulting over the moon when I should have been studying my Spelling."

Miss Pintake sucked her teeth noisily and shuffled the papers on her desk.

She looked at her watch and raised it to her ear.

"I'm a failure," thought Jessica sadly. "They will probably de-cloak me and make me return my Flying Licence. They might even take Berkeley away."

"I'm afraid I shall have to hurry you along," said Miss Pintake. "I've a very busy day…"

Jessica scratched her head – and that was when she had the idea. She started the rhyme again.

"Three Chocolate Mice,
Three Chocolate Mice,
See how they melt,
See how they melt,
They all run into the tablecloth,
It soaks them up with the chicken broth,
The gravy stains and the coffee froth…"

Then she flipped her cape over her shoulder and removed her helmet. With a dramatic flourish, she shook it several times

over Shar Pintake's desk and finished the
Spell triumphantly.

"Just give them a splat
With a wave of your hat
And they'll be THREE HEAD LICE.
THREE HEAD LICE!"

Shar Pintake noisily drew in her breath and hastily got to her feet. She had gone quite pale.

"Fine! Terrific! Marvellous!" she gabbled as she stamped PASSED on Jessica's Spelling Certificate and shooed her out of the door. "You know your way from here. Off you go. Chop chop."

The last thing Jessica saw as she closed the door was Shar Pintake peering suspiciously at her desk over her half-moon glasses.

"Too clever for her own good, that girl," she was muttering, "everyone else does the Warthog Spell."

Chapter Seven

Jessica was so excited. As a reward for passing her Spelling Test, Miss Strega was taking her to the theatre! Heckitty Darling, the famous actress witch, had sent two tickets for the opening night of her latest

show, *Snow White and the Seven Dwarfs*.

"And she has invited us to visit her backstage, at the interval," Miss Strega told Jessica as they took their seats in the Coven Garden theatre. They were right in the front row with a perfect view of the stage.

The lights went down. The curtain rose. As

Heckitty Darling glided into the spotlight, the audience went mad, cheering and clapping. Heckitty unclasped the owl brooch at her throat, theatrically threw her cape over her shoulder and blew kisses to everyone. As she caught sight of Jessica and Miss Strega, she made a deep curtsey.

"Even when she was a witch-in-training, I knew she was going to be a star," Miss Strega sighed and her chin bobbed up and down with emotion.

At the start of the show, Heckitty was the beautiful stepmother, with high heels that were as slender as needles and hair as black as ravens' feathers, who asked,

"Mirror, mirror, on the wall, who is the fairest one of all?"

But when she turned into the bad witch, she looked really scary. Her face was covered in boils. Her hair hung down to her shoulders in lanky greasy locks and she had a huge hump on her back. The first act ended when she persuaded Snow White to take a bite of the poisoned apple. There was a huge thunderclap. Snow White dropped silently to the floor. Heckitty Darling made a long

chilling cackle which made Jessica's hair stand on end and the curtain descended.

Jessica stood up at once. "Come on, Miss Strega, I can't wait to see Miss Darling."

But when they got backstage, they discovered that all was not well. There was a huddle of dwarfs standing at the door of Heckitty Darling's dressing room.

Snow White was wringing her hands. "I didn't trip her up deliberately. I just left the mop and bucket there..."

"And a very silly place it was to put a bucket, if I may say so!" declared Heckitty Darling, icily, from inside the room.

Miss Strega and Jessica pushed their way through the throng.

Heckitty Darling was sitting on the floor, in a puddle of water, groaning loudly, and rubbing her leg. "It's broken. How can I possibly be 'the fairest of them all' with a leg in plaster. I can just see the headlines on the W3 homepage: *Heckitty Darling Breaks Leg.*

Every witch on the web will cackle her head off."

"There, there," said Miss Strega soothingly. "I'm sure we can fix it."

"Not in time for the second act," Heckitty moaned and laid her wrist against her temple.

Miss Strega turned to Jessica, "What would Dr Krank do in these circumstances?"

"She might use her Withershins Ball and turn back the time so that Heckitty would not fall over the mop at all. Or she might give her a dose of General Purpose This-will-fix-it Brew and a spoonful of Cheery-ade."

"That's all well and good," murmured Heckitty, "but Dr Krank is not here, is she?"

Jessica smiled sweetly. "No, but I've just finished my Spelling Lessons. I think I know a Spell that might work."

Jessica knelt down on the floor beside

Heckitty and took her wand from her pocket. As Doc and Bashful and all the rest of the dwarfs looked on, she chanted:

"When you're feeling sort of broken,
Or bruised and out of sorts.
When your bones are acting funny,
And all your body hurts,
The Witch's Wand is your only friend."

Jessica's wand began to quiver in her hand as she moved it slowly along Miss Darling's leg. "Is it the knee? Not the knee. Is it the shinbone? The heelbone? The baby toe? The ankle?" At the last word, the wand trembled and glowed brightly. Jessica lightly tapped Heckitty's ankle.

There was a loud click. Snow White and the dwarfs gasped.

"Very impressive!" Heckitty Darling
exclaimed excitedly as Miss Strega and
Jessica helped her to her feet. "Take a bow!
You've fixed it!"

Jessica looked thrilled. "Wow, it worked!"

"Of course it worked!" said Miss Strega,

beaming from ear to ear. "After all, I taught you! And now I think you deserve another reward – don't you agree, my dear Miss Darling?"

Heckitty Darling pursed her lips and scrutinized Jessica from head to toe. "Indeed, I do, Miss Strega. And I know exactly what it ought to be. Would you both be so kind as to accompany me to the Wardrobe Department? We have just enough time before my curtain call."

The Wardrobe Department was a warren of treasure-filled rooms in the basement. There were crinolines and Roman breastplates, pantomime horses and huge feathery hats. There were scarecrows and lions' manes, Viking helmets and witches' brooms. Miss Wigg, the wardrobe mistress, was ironing Snow White's wedding dress. "Heckitty

Darling! And Miss Strega! What can I do for you?"

"Actually," said Miss Strega, "we're here for Jessica, my witch-in-training. She needs a new cloak."

"The special model, if possible," Heckitty added.

"You may be in luck," said Miss Wigg, tapping the side of her nose, for she too was a witch. She delved into a large wicker trunk and triumphantly pulled out a shiny black garment. "There we are," she said, draping it over Jessica's shoulders, "the Super-Duper De-Luxe Witch's Cape. Guaranteed-Invisibility-When-You-Need-It. *And* it's pure silk."

"Cool!" said Jessica, twirling around the room and occasionally disappearing among the costumes. "Thank you. Thank you."

"It's so *you*!" sighed Heckitty Darling as Jessica suddenly reappeared beside the wicker trunk.

Miss Strega steered Jessica towards the door. "Do stop disappearing, sweetheart. We all must fly. Heckitty's due back on stage in a few minutes and we must return to our seats."

Miss Wigg picked up her iron again. "That's a bright young trainee you have this year, Miss Strega. I suppose she's due to start Charming soon."

"Yes indeedy," said Miss Strega as she mounted her broomstick. "But where the dickens is she? Has she disappeared again?"

"I'm afraid so," said Miss Wigg. "Young witches never change, do they? Once they get their cloak of invisibility, they think they can just vanish into thin air."

Jessica chuckled inside her Super-Duper Cape. "I wonder what Charming will be about?" she thought. "I hope it's as much fun as Flying and Spelling."

And she reappeared at Miss Strega's side, ready for take-off.

Witch-in-Training
Flying Lessons

Maeve Friel

Illustrated by Nathan Reed

On Jessica's tenth birthday she discovers that she is a witch! With Miss Strega as her teacher, and a broomstick to fly, Jessica is ready to begin her training. The first book in a magical new series.

ISBN 0 00 713341 3

An imprint of HarperCollinsPublishers

www.roaringgoodreads.co.uk

Witch's the tears

Jenny Nimmo

Illustrated by Thierry Elfezzani

In freezing hail and howling wind, a stranger is given shelter at Theo's house – a stranger who loves telling stories and whose name is Mrs Scarum. Theo is convinced she's a witch and wishes his father would return home from his travels. But the blizzard continues and the night is long... there may be tears before morning.

ISBN 0 00 714162 9

ROARING GOOD READS

Collins

An imprint of HarperCollinsPublishers

www.roaringgoodreads.co.uk

Mr Skip

★ MICHAEL MORPURGO

ILLUSTRATED BY GRIFF

When Jackie finds a broken garden gnome in a
rubbish skip, she is determined to make him as good
as new. In return, Mister Skip makes Jackie's wishes
come true... almost! A fairy-tale for today from a
master storyteller.

ISBN 0 00 713474 6

ROARING GOOD READS

Collins

🏛 *An imprint of HarperCollinsPublishers*

www.roaringgoodreads.co.uk

Jean Ure

Illustrated by Karen Donnelly

For the first ten years of her life, Daisy lives in the Foundling Hospital with lots of other orphans. But on her tenth birthday she goes to work at the Dobell Academy for young ladies. There she watches, listens, learns and dreams. A 'rags-to-riches' story with a difference, where dreams really can come true!

ISBN 0 00 713369 3

≝ *An imprint of HarperCollinsPublishers*

www.roaringgoodreads.co.uk

Order Form

To order direct from the publishers, just make a list of the titles you want and fill in the form below:

Name ....

Address ....

....

....

Send to: Dept 6, HarperCollins Publishers Ltd, Westerhill Road, Bishopbriggs, Glasgow G64 2QT.

Please enclose a cheque or postal order to the value of the cover price, plus:

UK & BFPO: Add £1.00 for the first book, and 25p per copy for each additional book ordered.

Overseas and Eire: Add £2.95 service charge. Books will be sent by surface mail but quotes for airmail despatch will be given on request.

A 24-hour telephone ordering service is available to holders of Visa, MasterCard, Amex or Switch cards on 0141- 772 2281.

An imprint of HarperCollins*Publishers*